# Fancy NANCY

## Budding Ballerina

Based on *Fancy Nancy* written by Jane O'Connor

Cover illustration by Robin Preiss Glasser    Interior illustrations by Carolyn Bracken

HARPER FESTIVAL

*An Imprint of HarperCollinsPublishers*

Fancy Nancy: Budding Ballerina

Harper Festival is an imprint of HarperCollins Publishers.

Text copyright © 2013 by Jane O'Connor
Illustrations copyright © 2013 by Robin Preiss Glasser
Printed in the United States of America. All rights reserved.
No part of this book may be used or reproduced in any manner whatsoever without written permission except in the case of brief quotations embodied in critical articles and reviews.
For information address HarperCollins Children's books, a division of HarperCollins Publishers, 195 Broadway, New York, NY 10007.
www.harpercollinschildrens.com
Library of Congress catalog card number: 2012956504
ISBN 978-0-06-208628-0
Book design by Sean Boggs
14  15  16  17   CWM   10 9 8 7
❖
First Edition

I love ballet! My friend Bree and I go to class every week.
We do not dance on our toes yet. But one day we will. That is called
*en pointe.* (You say it like this: ahn pwant.)

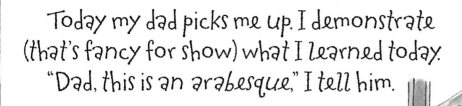

Today my dad picks me up. I demonstrate
(that's fancy for show) what I learned today.
"Dad, this is an arabesque," I tell him.

I *pirouette*—that's like twirling—into the house.
Frenchy wags her tail. That's her way of *telling* me how graceful I am.

"Dad, you *pirouette* now," I suggest.

Dad tries his best. Oops!

"I'm not a natural dancer like you are," Dad tells me.
"Dad, you must have a positive attitude."
That means he has to believe in himself.

"You just need to start with simpler stuff."

Ooh la la! Suddenly I have a stupendous idea.

My mom and JoJo come home.

I show the class how to do second, third, and fourth positions.

By the time we get to fifth position, my dad's legs are all tangled up.

"It's okay, Dad," I say. "You are making progress—that's fancy for getting better."

Just then the doorbell rings. I tell my students that they may take a break. Then I answer the door. It's Bree! Now I have another stupendous idea....

"You have all worked hard, especially Dad. Now we will perform for you," I tell the class. "Watch and learn."

We plié (You say it like this: plee-ay)...

...we jeté (You say it like this: je-tay)...

...and we do many *pirouettes*.

"Bravo!" everyone cheers.

Later I get out my glitter pens again. "Here, Dad," I tell him. "You earned this. You're the real budding ballerina."